MELVIN BEEDERMAN SUPERHERO

www.melvinbeederman.com

MELVIN BEEDERMAN SUPERHERO

THE FAKE CAPE CAPER

GREG TRINE

ILLUSTRATED BY
RHODE MONTIJO

HENRY HOLT AND COMPANY ★ NEW YORK

To my brother Tom
—G. T.

For my super friends: One Hit Wonder,
The Human Piñata, and Master Mime
—R. M.

Henry Holt and Company, LLC
Publishers since 1866
175 Fifth Avenue, New York, New York 10010
www.HenryHoltKids.com

Henry Holt® is a registered trademark of Henry Holt and Company, LLC.
Text copyright © 2007 by Greg Trine
Illustrations copyright © 2007 by Rhode Montijo
All rights reserved. Distributed in Canada by H. B. Fenn and Company Ltd.

Library of Congress Cataloging-in-Publication Data
Trine, Greg.
The fake cape caper / Greg Trine; art by Rhode Montijo.—1st ed.
p.   cm. — (Melvin Beederman, superhero)
Summary: Melvin Beederman, superhero in charge of Los Angeles,
attends the Superhero Convention in Las Vegas, leaving his young
sidekick to keep Los Angeles safe from evil bad guys and bullies.
ISBN-13: 978-08050-8158-9 / ISBN-10: 0-8050-8158-5 (hardcover)
3 5 7 9 10 8 6 4 2

ISBN-13: 978-08050-8159-6 / ISBN-10: 0-8050-8159-3 (paperback)
3 5 7 9 10 8 6 4

[1. Heroes—Fiction. 2. Los Angeles (Calif.)—Fiction. 3. Humorous stories.]
I. Montijo, Rhode, ill. II. Title.
PZ7.T7356Fak 2007   [Fic]—dc22   2006036355

First Edition—2007
Hand-lettering by David Gatti
Printed in May 2010 in the United States of America by
R. R. Donnelley & Sons Company, Harrisonburg, Virginia

CONTENTS

SUPERHERO CONVENTION

Superhero Melvin Beederman was sitting on top of City Hall, taking a break. It had been a busy morning of catching bad guys, sinister sleazeballs, and devious dudes . . . not to mention devious dames. Twelve drug dealers, seven car thieves, two bank robbers, and one guy who was just thinking about taking over the world. He had that I'm-thinking-of-taking-over-the-world look on his face. Melvin had seen that expression before, and he decided to put a stop to it before it got out of hand.

But now it was break time, or rather lunchtime, and Melvin sat eating pretzels and drinking root beer on top of one of the tallest buildings in Los Angeles. "This is my town," he said to himself as he looked around. It was. Melvin was the superhero in charge of L.A. Along with his sidekick Candace Brinkwater, he kept the peace and lunched on top of tall buildings as often as possible.

Suddenly one of the pretzels started ringing.

Melvin jumped. "Holy high-tech snack food. I forgot all about my pretzel phone."

Holy high-tech snack food, indeed! He did forget.

Melvin had purchased the pretzel phone at Sneaky Sam's Gadgets for Good Guys. As everyone knows, Sneaky Sam has been providing crime-fighting tools to California's secret agents and superheroes since 1942.

The pretzel phone rang again, and Melvin answered it. "Hello. Melvin Beederman here."

"Melvin! This is Superhero James."

"James!" Melvin was so excited he almost fell off the building. Almost.

James had been one of Melvin's best friends back at the Superhero Academy. "What's up? Catch any bad guys lately?"

"More than I can count."

"I know what you mean," Melvin said, although he always counted them.

"Listen, Melvin, I called to see if you are going to the Superhero Convention in Las Vegas."

"Superhero Convention? What about my day job? I'm in charge of Los Angeles, you know." Melvin took saving the world seriously.

"Put your sidekick in charge for a few days," James suggested. "That's what Margaret and I are doing."

Superhero Margaret was Melvin's other best friend from the Superhero Academy. Melvin hadn't seen either of them in months. Going to Las Vegas sounded pretty great. A Superhero Convention sounded even better. And seeing his best friends in the whole world sounded best of all.

"What do you say, Melvin buddy?"

Melvin wasn't sure if his sidekick Candace Brinkwater could handle the job. After all, she had not graduated from the academy. She was just the girl with whom he had decided to divide his cape, and this was all because of a mistake made at the dry cleaners. Could she handle Los Angeles all by herself? It was hard to say. What if Max the Wonder Thug went on a crime spree? Or Calamity Wayne, for that matter?

Still, he really wanted to see James and Margaret.

Melvin decided to go for it and hope for the best. "I'll be there," he said. "When is it?"

"It starts tomorrow and lasts all week. Didn't you get a flyer in the mail?"

"I live in a tree house, James. I don't exactly have an address."

This was true. Melvin lived in a tree house overlooking the city. From there he could spot crimes before they happened, and occasionally catch guys who were just thinking about doing devious or sinister deeds—like taking over the world.

"See you in Vegas," James said.

"Yeah, see you there." Melvin hung up the pretzel. He was still hungry and had the sudden urge to eat his phone. Instead he put it in his pocket so he wouldn't be tempted. Then he looked at his watch. Three o'clock.

"Holy I'm-late-to-help-Candace-with-her-math-homework!" Melvin said. He stood up and dusted pretzel crumbs off his cape.

Holy he's-late-to-help-Candace-with-her-math-homework, indeed! Melvin met Candace every day at the library to tutor her in math. Then they teamed up to save the world. This was their arrangement, and so far it was working.

"Up, up, and away," Melvin said and jumped from the top of City Hall.

Crash!

He hit the ground hard. Very hard. After all, it was a long way down.

He tried again. "Up, up, and away."

Splat!

Two more times.

Thud!

Kabonk!

On the fifth try he was up and flying. This was the way it went with Melvin. He hardly ever got off the ground in one try.

He headed for the library, looking down at the city below. He saw thousands of people—and thousands of pairs of underwear. Melvin couldn't turn off his x-ray vision. He saw underwear everywhere he looked.

"Try not to think about it, " he told himself. "I just ate. "

Yes, Melvin, you do that. Throwing up from that height would be disgusting. Plus, it would get this book dirty.

CANDACE IN CHARGE

This is how a normal person sees a crowded library.

This is how Melvin Beederman sees it.

Notice the underwear? So did Melvin.
It was just after three when he arrived
at the library. Candace was waiting for
him at their usual table. "You're late,"
she said.

"Sorry." Melvin sat down beside her. "Lost track of time."

"No problem. I never feel like doing math."

"I know."

They got down to work anyway. After all, the world needed saving, and the two partners in uncrime couldn't do that until Candace finished her math. When she did, they launched themselves outside the library, which was fine with Melvin. He was getting awfully tired of seeing the librarian's yellow underwear. Melvin didn't care what anyone said—yellow underwear just seemed suspicious.

"Up, up, and away," they said together.

Candace soared above the treetops.

Not Melvin.

Crash!

Splat!

Thud!

Kabonk!

He joined Candace in the air on the fifth try. "Sorry it took so long," he told her.

"No problem." Candace had pulled a paperback out of her pocket and was reading as she hovered above the trees. As long as she had to wait for Melvin to launch himself, she may as well get some reading done.

"Put that thing away, Candace. Let's go save the world."

Candace slid the book into her back pocket. "Right."

They zoomed. They really zoomed!

As they sped across the sky, Candace

looked at Melvin. "How fast do you think we're going?" she asked.

"A hundred miles an hour at least. Why do you ask?"

"I was just wondering why your hair never moves, even when you're going a hundred miles an hour."

"It's the illustrator," Melvin said.

"What?"

"Yeah, I don't draw my hair like this. It's the illustrator."

"Hmm," Candace said. "That's weird."

"Not as weird as you having only four fingers."

Candace looked at her hand. "What do you mean?"

"Count them," Melvin said. "Three fingers and a thumb."

"That is weird. You know what else is weird, Melvin?"

"What?"

"You have only three fingers and a thumb, too."

The two partners in uncrime sped across the sky, looking at their hands and wondering why they didn't have fingers like most humans. They wondered why the illustrator drew them that way. They wondered if all superheroes were missing a finger. They wondered if it was a good idea to travel a hundred miles an hour and not look where they were going.

"Melvin, look out!"

SPLAT!

They crashed into the wall of the very building where Melvin had had lunch—City Hall—and hit the ground a few seconds later.

Candace slowly got to her feet. "So that's what it feels like to go splat."

"Yes," Melvin said, "that's what it

feels like, all right. How do you like it?"

"I don't."

Melvin suddenly remembered about the Superhero Convention in Las Vegas. Hitting buildings doing one hundred miles per hour always affected his memory in one way or another. Usually it made him forget. This time it made him remember.

He turned to Candace. "How would you like to be in charge of Los Angeles for a while?"

Candace stopped brushing herself off. "In charge?"

"Yes," Melvin said, "in charge. Not Candace Brinkwater, the Superhero assistant, but Candace Brinkwater, Superhero."

Candace thought this over. She'd never been in charge of anything before, except maybe cleaning her room. And once she was reader of the day at school. But to be in charge of a whole city? All by herself? She was just a third-grader in a cape!

"I have to go to the Superhero Convention in Las Vegas," Melvin told her. "I'm leaving you in charge. What do you say, Candace? Are you game?"

Candace was silent a moment. She looked at the tall buildings around her. A whole city all to herself, which was better than being in charge of a bedroom any day. "I'll do it," she said finally. "Count me in, Melvin."

Later that evening, Melvin watched *The Adventures of Thunderman* with his pet rat Hugo. It was their favorite show. They loved how Thunderman and his assistant Thunder Thighs saved the world in every single episode.

When it was over Melvin called Candace on his pretzel phone. "I lied about my hair," he told her.

"What do you mean?"

"It's not the illustrator that makes my hair stay in one place when I fly."

"What is it then?"

"Melvin Mousse."

MELVIN GOES TO VEGAS

Melvin's pet rat Hugo was one hungry rodent. He sat flipping channels on the TV, looking for an episode or two of *The Adventures of Thunderman*, and eating pretzels. One of them was very crunchy. Of course, this was no ordinary pretzel. Hugo had eaten Melvin's pretzel phone by mistake. Melvin didn't know this until his rat started ringing.

Without thinking, he picked up Hugo

and said, "Hello." Suddenly he realized that he was speaking into a rat's belly button. "Hugo, what did you do?"

"Squeak," said the rat.

This meant either "Your phone looked too good to resist" or "Care to join me in a grilled cheese sandwich?" Melvin was never exactly sure about rat talk.

He still had the rat to his ear and could hear Candace speaking. It was a little muffled with all the rat fur, but he could tell it was his partner in uncrime.

"Just wanted to say have fun and don't worry about your day job," Candace said. "I'll take care of our town."

"I know you will, Candace. I'll see you in a few days."

"Are you feeling okay? You sound a little muffled."

Hugo's fur was starting to tickle Melvin's cheek. "It's a long story," he said. Pet rats can be so annoying.

Melvin packed his suitcase and said

good-bye to Hugo. He was so excited about seeing his best friends again that he launched himself from the tree house without climbing down first.

Well, you know what happened.

Crash!

He also tore his cape on a piece of splintery wood on the tree house door. Melvin got to his feet and looked up. Hugo was looking down and holding a small piece of cape that had torn off.

"Squeakity squeak," the rat said.

This meant "This will make a good comforter for my bed." Or it might have been "Bring me back one of those crunchy pretzels."

Melvin didn't stick around to figure what Hugo was saying. He launched himself again. "Up, up, and away."

Four tries later he was up and flying. He streaked across the sky toward Las Vegas and his two best friends in the world. It would be great to see them again. And the Superhero Convention sounded cool, too. James had e-mailed Melvin all about it after they'd spoken on the phone. Yesterday's Bully, Tomorrow's Bad Guy was one of the classes offered at the convention, because knowing your enemy was always a good idea. Other classes were Train Stopping Made Easy and Overcoming Your Weakness or at Least Living with It.

If only they had a class called Turning Off Your X-ray Vision, Melvin thought as he flew. It would be nice not to see underwear everywhere he looked.

Melvin made it to Las Vegas and checked into the hotel. He had no clue that the Superhero Convention was not the only meeting in town. Directly across the street, at the Hotel del Lunatic, they were having the Evil Bad Guys Convention, where they offered classes like Yesterday's Math Genius, Tomorrow's Superhero, because knowing your enemy was always a good idea. Other classes included Finding Your Enemy's Weakness and What to Do When They Can See Your Underwear. Bad guys hated when you could see their underwear.

There was also a class called Perfecting Your Evil Laugh, which is a skill all criminals needed. If you're a bad guy and you can't laugh evilly, you'd better find another line of work.

Melvin met his friends Superhero Margaret and Superhero James for pretzels and root beer. Little did they know that right across the street there were bad guys with sinister and devious things on their minds. Some of them were even thinking of taking over the world!

MEANWHILE . . .

While Melvin was busy in Las Vegas at the Superhero Convention, Candace held down the fort in Los Angeles. The first morning after Melvin left, Candace got up early for school. She attended Highmont Ridge Elementary School. The bullies had been acting up again, doing deeds that were not quite devious and sinister—but almost. As everyone knows, yesterday's bullies become tomorrow's bad guys, and Candace knew she had to act fast to put things back in order.

"I have to act fast," she said. Candace also knew she wasn't supposed to repeat what the narrator says, but sometimes she just couldn't help herself.

"I can't help—"

That's enough of that, Candace.

"Oh, sorry."

Candace kissed her mom good-bye, grabbed her books, and took off for school. And she really took off . . . right from her front porch.

"Up, up, and away." She was up and flying in one try as usual. Then she zoomed over her neighborhood to Highmont Ridge Elementary School.

The bullies were already at it—some of them had decided to get an early start also. Johnny Fink, Highmont's biggest bully, was holding a second-grader upside down by the ankles.

His best buddy, Knucklehead Wilson, scooped up all the lunch money falling out of the kid's pockets.

Candace flew to the rescue. "Ahem," she said. "Unhand that boy."

Unhand that boy? According to the Superhero Code, you were supposed to say "Not so fast!" when you came upon the bad guys. But of course Candace didn't know the code because she hadn't graduated from the academy. She just said the first thing that popped into her head.

"Unhand that boy?" Johnny Fink said. He and Knucklehead laughed. Even they knew that wasn't real superhero talk.

"Yes," Candace said. "Unhand him, or I'll do it for you."

The two boys laughed harder. At least they did until Candace grabbed them. They were not laughing at all when she dragged them to the principal's office.

After school, in detention, Johnny looked at Knucklehead and said,

"Something's got to be done about Candace Brinkwater."

"I know," said Knucklehead. "Got any ideas?"

"It's her cape, Knucklehead. She didn't have superpowers before she started wearing the cape."

"If only your dad hadn't divided Melvin Beederman's cape."

"I know." Johnny's father was none other than Milo the Wonder Tailor. No one would go to a tailor called Fink, so he changed his name. He was responsible for making Candace's cape out of part of Melvin's. "It's all my dad's fault. If only he hadn't—"

Johnny stopped and gave Knucklehead a sly smile.

"Do you have an idea?" Knucklehead asked.

"Not yet, but something's brewing up there." Johnny tapped his noggin. Not head—noggin.

"Trouble?"

"Could be. Meet me at the fort after dinner."

The two boys didn't have a hideout or a lair. It was just a fort. But it was a good place to make plans, and that was all that mattered.

"Candace Brinkwater, your superhero days are numbered," Johnny said with almost an evil laugh. Almost. He'd have to work on it if he was ever going to make the jump from bully to full-fledged bad guy. You just can't be all that evil without an evil laugh.

But Johnny didn't care. He had too much on his mind. One way or another, he had to get his hands on Candace Brinkwater's cape.

A SPAZ OR TWO

Melvin was glad to be in Las Vegas. It was good to see his best friends, Superhero James and Superhero Margaret. They had all signed up for the same classes and were really looking forward to perfecting some of their hero skills, especially Melvin.

"How's the underwear thing going?" James asked. "Have you been able to turn off the x-ray vision yet?"

Melvin shook his head. "No. And by

36

the way, your striped ones look great."

"And the train stopping?" Margaret asked. "How's that going?"

"Still struggling," Melvin said. Ever since the Superhero Academy he'd had difficulty stopping speeding locomotives. "It's a good thing bad guys don't escape by train very often. I can stop cars and buses just fine. And I have no problem at all with skateboards."

The three superheroes hung out at the convention, browsing the booths that displayed the very latest in cape design and had books on everything from Choosing the Perfect Sidekick to Overcoming Your Enemy's Evil Laugh. They also had a variety of gadgets in the form of snack foods. Melvin bought another pretzel phone and called Candace with it.

"How's it going, Candace?" Melvin asked. He had a fierce desire to eat his phone. He resisted it. "Any bad guy problems?"

"No major ones so far—mostly school bullies. I can handle them."

"Okay. If you need me just call me on my pretzel." Melvin hung up. He still felt a little strange about leaving his partner in uncrime in charge of Los Angeles. But then again, James and Margaret had done the same. James was the superhero in charge of Atlanta. Margaret was in charge of Saint Paul. If their sidekicks could do the job, then so could Candace.

Or could she?

Sure, she was the only one ever to score 500 points in a single game of basketball. Sure, she ran the hundred-yard dash in three and a half seconds. And she was the only third-grader who could fly. But Melvin was worried anyway. Something didn't feel right.

James looked at Melvin. "You have that something-is-not-right look on your face." They were taught how to read faces at the Superhero Academy. James was an expert. "You worry too much. Everything is fine."

Little did James know! Melvin's instincts were correct. Trouble was brewing. But it wasn't brewing in Los Angeles—not yet anyway. It was brewing across the street, at the Evil Bad Guys Convention. Sinister and devious plots were being hatched right and left. There were no less than six take-over-the-world plans going on at the same time. Fortunately none of them involved Los Angeles. What did affect L.A. was that two bad guys spotted Melvin Beederman as he was walking down the street with James and Margaret.

"Don't look now," one of the bad guys said, "but I think that's Melvin Beederman."

The other bad guy turned his head.

"I said don't look now!"

These were the Spaz Brothers, Major and his brother, Big. Everybody thought Major was the leader, but it was really Big. They had both flunked out of mad scientist school and decided to become evil bad guys instead. And now they were at the Bad Guys Convention, brushing up on their evil laughs, among other things.

"Hee ha hee ha ha hee." Major had a long way to go in the evil laugh department. "Melvin Beederman? That's him?"

"Yes," said Big. "And do you know what that means?"

"Not exactly."

"It means if Melvin is here, who is watching over Los Angeles?"

Major thought about this. "Nobody?"

"Exactly. What do you say we head to L.A.?"

"Hee ha hee ha ha hee."

Big knew that his brother needed help with his evil laugh. But he had other things on his mind—evil things. Los Angeles was in trouble.

So was Candace.

JOHNNY FINK'S EVIL PLAN

There were a lot of evil plans going around—take-over-the-world plans, bank robbery plans, cheating-on-test plans—but the one closest to Candace Brinkwater was the one being hatched by Johnny Fink and his faithful bullying companion Knucklehead Wilson.

They were in their underground fort. Johnny paced back and forth. Knucklehead sat on the beanbag chair in the corner. "So what's your idea?" Knucklehead said.

Johnny stopped. An evil grin crossed his face. He was years away from perfecting his evil laugh, but he had the grin thing down perfectly. "I say we steal Candace Brinkwater's cape."

"How are we going to do that?" Knucklehead said. "Haven't you noticed? She's stronger than us. She can run fast. She can fly. She can see our underwear!"

"No, that's Melvin Beederman. Candace doesn't have x-ray vision problems."

"Still, she's a superhero. How are we going to get her cape?"

"I'm not sure yet," Johnny said. "We have to investigate."

That night Johnny waited until everyone in the Fink household was asleep, then he snuck out of his bedroom window and met Knucklehead at their fort.

"Do you know where Candace lives?" Knucklehead asked. They were dressed in dark clothes and had black stuff on their faces. They weren't full-fledged bad guys yet, but they sure felt like it.

"Yes," Johnny said. "I have a map. Follow me."

The two partners in bullying stayed in the shadows as they made their way to Candace's house. All the lights were out at her place, but the moon provided plenty of light. They looked in every window until they found Candace's room. There was a gap in the curtains so they could look inside.

"Drat!" Johnny whispered.

"Don't you mean 'curses'?"

"No, I'm not a full-fledged bad guy. I'm just a school bully." Johnny hoped to

be a real bad guy someday, but he was not there yet and he knew it. He pointed into Candace's room. "She wears her cape to bed."

"Then we won't be able to steal it," Knucklehead said.

"Sure we will. It just won't be as easy. I have a plan."

The next day at school Johnny and Knucklehead watched Candace carefully. Mostly, they watched her cape. While everyone was supposed to be working on math, the two boys drew pictures of the cape, the one created by Johnny's own father, Milo the Wonder Tailor. If they could duplicate the cape, they could switch it with the real one while Candace was sleeping.

At least Johnny thought they could.

Knucklehead wasn't so sure. As long as she had on the cape, she had super-powers. "What if Candace wakes up, Johnny? She'll beat us up just like she always does."

"I'm willing to take that risk." Johnny had his evil grin again. It was even better than before. One day he'd start working on his evil laugh, but not right now. He had too much to do. He had to get the cape. When he did, he'd be in control of Highmont Ridge Elementary School.

And Candace Brinkwater would be powerless to do anything about it.

MEANWHILE . . .

While the school bullies plotted to get Candace's cape, and while Melvin attended the Superhero Convention, Major Spaz and his brother, Big, made plans to go to Los Angeles, the place they thought had no superhero protecting it. The problem was that they had no car and they had spent their last dime on the Evil Bad Guys Convention.

"We spent our last dime on the Evil Bad Guys Convention," said Big.

They didn't know that they weren't supposed to repeat what the narrator says. In fact, this was the first time they were in a book.

"So what do we do?" Major asked.

"We're bad guys, aren't we?" Big said. "We do what bad guys do."

"You mean we take over the world?" Major smiled. He'd heard of people trying to take over the world, but he'd never actually done it.

"No, we steal a car so we can get to Los Angeles."

But stealing a car wasn't easy, especially for two guys who flunked out of mad scientist school. Nobody left cars unlocked with the keys inside. And their attempts at hot-wiring resulted in stereos blaring and alarms going off.

How to get to Los Angeles? That was the question. Could they find a way to get there without stealing a car?

Their chance came when they overheard two truckers discussing cargo. The truckers were taking a bunch of mannequins to be delivered to a Hollywood movie studio. As the truck was being loaded, Major and Big joined the group of mannequins.

"Okay. Now what do we do?" Major whispered.

"Just stand there and make like a dummy."

No problem there. Major Spaz had been doing this all of his life. He wasn't any good at being a mad scientist, but he was an expert at being a dummy.

The plan worked. The two truckers loaded all the mannequins onto the truck, including the bad-guy additions. Neither

of the truckers noticed that two of their cargo were living, though they wondered why a Hollywood movie studio would want such ugly props.

"Did you see those last two?" one of the truckers asked.

"Yeah. Pretty ugly if you ask me," said the other.

"They smell bad, too."

It wasn't part of the Bad Guy's Code to smell bad, but it was very common.

The two truckers shut the rear door of the truck and hopped in the cab. Then they headed for Hollywood, which was right next to Los Angeles, the place Melvin had left unprotected.

Once inside the truck, Big Spaz looked at his brother and said, "Okay, Major, you can relax now. No one's looking."

Major let out his breath and relaxed.

"I said you can stop making like a dummy."

"I did," Major said.

"Really? How strange."

It was hard to tell when Major was making like a dummy and when he wasn't.

FAST TIMES . . . VERY FAST TIMES

Every year Highmont Ridge Elementary School held a mini Olympic games. There was a tetherball tournament, basketball games, track-and-field events. You name it, they had it.

But this was the first year Highmont had a superhero. Candace Brinkwater signed up for track-and-field to see if she could break her own record of three and a half seconds in the hundred-yard dash.

She also signed up for basketball to see if she could score more than 500 points in a single game. This was also her record.

As luck would have it (or maybe it was unluck), Johnny Fink was in both the hundred-yard dash and basketball. He had to go up against Candace . . . gulp . . . twice . . . gulp gulp.

The track-and-field events were first. Johnny and Candace stood side by side for the hundred-yard dash.

"On your mark." A teacher pointed a pistol in the air.

Johnny, Candace, and six other kids got ready.

Knucklehead cheered for his partner in bullying. "Let's go, Johnny. Three and a half seconds is doable."

Maybe it was doable for a superhero, but it sure wasn't for Johnny.

"Get set."

Everyone crouched, ready to spring when the gun went off.

Bang!

Candace ran so fast she nearly left the ground. Fast as a speeding bullet. Maybe faster. The track smoked. So did her shoes! It was fast times at Highmont Ridge.

Fast times, indeed! When the other runners arrived at the finish line, Candace was busy eating a hotdog and thinking of her next event. Basketball.

Knucklehead patted his buddy on the back. "You came in second, Johnny. Not bad."

Johnny snorted. Losing to Candace just made him madder. He was more determined than ever to get her cape.

Next it was basketball, Candace and her team against Johnny and Knucklehead's. Each team had five players, but it was all Candace. She was everywhere at once, which isn't difficult when you're as fast as a speeding bullet. She blocked shots, stole passes, shot from the outside, from the inside—she slam-dunked.

Candace's team, 132; Johnny's team, 6.

The second quarter was even worse!

A crowd had gathered to watch the slaughter. Candace dribbled the ball behind her back, between her legs, put up a shot. *Swish!* People in the neighborhood watched from the fence. The school janitor stopped what he was doing and came over, as did the school nurse. It was showtime and Candace Brinkwater was the main attraction.

Slam . . . swish . . . slam . . . slam.

Johnny and Knucklehead walked away defeated. They were sweaty and bruised. Their feet hurt, which, of course, is what the agony of de-feet is all about.

"We have to put a stop to Candace Brinkwater," Johnny said. "We have to get the cape away from her."

Knucklehead nodded, looking at his sore feet. "I know."

"Tonight," Johnny said.

"Tonight?" Knucklehead gulped.

"Yes." Johnny's evil grin was back. "Operation: Cape-Switch."

THE SPAZ BROTHERS

The road to Los Angeles was long, hot, and boring for Major Spaz and his brother, Big. It was so boring that Major struck up a conversation with a nearby mannequin. "Come here often?"

The mannequin didn't reply. She just stood there with a blank look on her face.

Big Spaz was so bored that he started singing. "The long and boring road . . ."

When the truck got to Los Angeles, Major stopped talking and Big stopped singing. Just in time. Just in the nick of time, to be exact. Sometimes even bad guys did things in the nick of time. The rear door began to open.

"Quick, Major," Big whispered. "Make like a dummy again!"

Truth be told, Major was always pretty close to dummy-mode.

The two bad guys stood motionless as they were carried off the truck. When the truckers turned their backs, Major and Big ran.

"Hey," one of the truckers said a little later, "what ever happened to those ugly mannequins?"

"You mean the smelly ones?"

"Yeah."

"I'm not sure, but aren't you glad to be rid of them?"

The other trucker nodded, and the two of them continued unloading the truck.

"Hee ha hee ha ha hee. Did you see that, Big? Those truckers didn't even miss us."

You can say that again!

Major Spaz had a long way to go in perfecting his evil laugh. He should have stayed at the Evil Bad Guys Convention so he could work on it. But no matter. The brothers were on their own now, in a town with no superhero guarding it. Or so they thought. Little did they know that Candace Brinkwater was on the job.

"What do we do now?" Major asked.

Big gave his brother a tired look. "We find a lair, of course. What kind of bad guy are you?"

Major didn't answer this question. He had already flunked out of mad scientist school. He didn't have to be told he was a lousy bad guy.

But where do you look for a lair? Big thought. *And how do you get one with no money?*

Fortunately, they were standing beneath a billboard advertising Big Al's

Rent-a-Lair. And Big Al was having
a special—no payment
for ninety days.

"We'll have a few bank jobs under our belts by then, Major."

They went to Big Al's, looked around, and settled for a lair with a Jacuzzi. It was delivered later that day to a vacant lot on top of a hill, which was right next to a tree house with a funny-looking **M** on the side. The tree house looked empty, though Major and Big thought they saw a rat standing in the doorway and eating pretzels.

The brothers settled into their new home.

"What's next?" Major asked as he cannonballed into the Jacuzzi.

Big was looking out over the city, thinking of their first job. Should they rob a bank, heist some jewelry, steal a car? So many crimes, so little time.

"We need transportation before we can commit any decent crimes," Big said. This was not part of the Bad Guy's Code, but it made sense to Big. "Let's steal a car, Major."

They had no luck doing this in Las Vegas, of course, but with their new lair and a new city spread out before them, something told them their luck was about to change.

Someday maybe they'd try to take over the world. But for now, they'd settle for stealing a car.

THE CAPE CAPER

Johnny Fink lived with his family in a little apartment above his father's shop— his father who was none other than Milo the Wonder Tailor. It was Milo who had divided Melvin Beederman's cape in two, which made Candace Brinkwater into a notorious sidekick and all-around good girl . . . and pretty darn good superhero.

Johnny waited until everyone was sound asleep. Then he went downstairs and opened the front door of the shop,

where Knucklehead Wilson was waiting.

"Got the drawings?" Johnny asked.

Knucklehead unzipped his jacket and pulled out some papers. He handed them to Johnny.

"Perfect. Let's get to work."

On the papers were the sketches they'd made of Candace's cape. Now to make a copy of it.

The two boys kept the lights off and worked by flashlight, just in case Johnny's father woke up. If he did, it would be easier to douse the light and hide.

Milo the Wonder Tailor didn't wake up. This gave the boys all night to work on the fake cape. And work they did. Everything was a flurry of red cloth, thread, and scissors.

Knucklehead stood on a stool to model
the finished product.

"How do I look?"

"Good enough to hate," Johnny said with his evil grin spreading across his face.

Knucklehead jumped off the stool and looked at himself in the mirror. "Holy I-look-just-like-Candace."

Holy what-was-he-talking-about? He didn't look anything like Candace. He was a lot uglier. But the cape looked like the real one, and that was all that mattered.

Johnny checked the time. They had a few hours before the sun would be up. "We still have time to make the switch, Knucklehead. Let's go."

The two boys made their way to Candace's house.

"I still don't understand how we're going to do it," Knucklehead said. "She'll be wearing her cape. If she wakes up, we're history."

Johnny didn't say anything. It was hard to keep his evil grin in place and talk at the same time. Besides, he needed to think. How would they get the cape away from Candace, the girl who was more powerful than a speeding loco-motive? The girl who could bench-press a Buick? The girl who could fly?

They got to the house and peered through the gap in the curtains of Candace's room. She was sound asleep. Johnny tried the window. It was locked. But the next one was open. He slid it up and climbed inside, holding a finger to his lips. Knucklehead followed.

They stood in a dark room and waited

for their eyes to adjust. Candace's parents were asleep. Johnny and Knucklehead crept into the hall, which was lit by a night-light.

Suddenly they stopped. Candace Brinkwater was standing in the hall, looking their way!

THE SPAZ-MOBILE

Major Spaz and his brother, Big, sat in their Jacuzzi until late into the night. They weren't used to such luxury, and so they made good use of it. Plus they had to wait for most of Los Angeles to go to sleep before they could make their move. And what was this move? To steal a car, of course. Or at least something with wheels. They weren't all that picky.

It was way past midnight when they crawled out of the Jacuzzi.

"Holy wrinkled bad guy," Big said, looking at himself in a full-length mirror. "That water did a number on us, Major."

Holy wrinkled bad guy, indeed! It sure did. Here a wrinkle, there a wrinkle, everywhere a wrinkle wrinkle.

Major looked at his reflection and nodded.

The Spaz Brothers put on their bad-guy clothes and went out. Once again, they thought they saw a pretzel-eating rat in a nearby tree.

The question was, What kind of car to steal? What exactly was the perfect bad-guy vehicle? Something fast, of course, but also something that didn't stand out in a crowd.

The Spaz Brothers walked down a dark street, checking car doors. Every last one of them was locked. And Major and Big had decided not to try hot-wiring anything. They'd tried that in Las

Vegas and got nothing but screaming car alarms and blaring stereos.

What to do?

They found a car lot on Grand Avenue. Lots of big cars. But also one big dog guarding the place. They moved on.

"We'll have to hijack a car," Big said finally.

"How are we going to do that? We don't have a gun."

Big headed for the nearest intersection, where there was a stoplight. "Just follow my lead, and whatever you do, do not, I repeat, do not use your evil laugh."

The brothers hid in the bushes near the stoplight. When a car came to a stop, they ran up to it and Big yelled, "GET OUT OF THE CAR!"

The driver did. He got out and left the motor running. He'd never seen such wrinkled bad guys before and it scared him.

Big and Major jumped in the car and took off.

"Holy car stealing!" Major said. "That was too easy."

Holy car stealing, indeed! It was. But, of course, it was the wrinkles. Trust me.

The brothers wasted no time in committing more crimes. They had a lair payment coming up in just ninety days. They had to get busy.

And they did. They robbed a liquor store on Melville. Not Melvin; Melville. They crashed through the front window of a jewelry store and grabbed handfuls of jewels. Then they held up a pizza delivery guy, because all those sinister and devious deeds made for mighty hungry bad guys.

"Now can I use my evil laugh?" Major said as they headed back to the lair.

Big groaned. He knew Major wouldn't be able to sleep if he didn't get it out of his system. "Okay, go on."

"Hee ha hee ha ha hee." Major smiled. Now he could go to sleep knowing he had put in a good night's work and topped it off properly—with his laugh.

HUGO THE SPY

Hugo missed Melvin something awful. He missed him coming home after a long day of saving the world. He missed having someone to watch *The Adventures of Thunderman* and eat pretzels with.

Speaking of pretzels, Hugo had eaten so many that his stomach started to feel funny. It also rang now and then. And sometimes it seemed to be talking to him, saying the same thing over and

over: "If you'd like to make a call, please hang up and try again. If you need help, hang up and then dial the operator. If you'd like to make a call . . ."

It was very hard to sleep with all that going on in his stomach. Fortunately, there was plenty happening in the neighborhood to keep him interested. A house had just gone up next door, and whoever lived there must have been having trouble sleeping, too. Late into the night Hugo could hear *pitter patter pitter patter pitter patter*, then "Geronimo!" *kersplash!* Sometimes it was "Wheeee!" *kersplash!* Other times it was "Cowabunga!" *kersplash*. The *kersplash* part never changed.

Hugo watched and listened from the door of the tree house. When the kersplashing stopped, he saw two very wrinkled guys leave the place next door. *Kind of late to be going for a stroll,* he thought. He decided he'd better keep eye on Wrinkled One and Wrinkled Two.

Hugo had dozed off after his neighbors left. But then his stomach started ringing and talking to him. He was wide awake when they returned a few hours later— this time in a car. Hugo watched carefully.

Wrinkled One and Wrinkled Two carried bags into the house, and one of them was saying, "Hee ha hee ha ha hee." Maybe he had something stuck in his throat and was trying to cough it out. Hugo didn't know. But those bags looked suspicious . . . very suspicious.

"Squeaker squeak squeaken," the rat said to himself. This meant "If I didn't

know better, I'd say there was loot in those bags" (not money—loot). Or maybe it was "I wish my stomach would shut up."

In any case, Hugo, the Superhero pet, decided to keep an eye out for more suspicious deeds. He knew that suspicious deeds were just a step away from sinister and devious ones. And since Melvin was not around to take care of things, he would.

SORRY TO LEAVE YOU HANGING . . .

Johnny Fink and Knucklehead Wilson were in the hall at Candace Brinkwater's house. But they weren't the only ones. Candace was there, too, looking right at them.

"We're history," Knucklehead whispered. "What do we do?"

There was nothing they could do, of course. And Johnny knew this. Candace was faster than them. She was stronger. She could bench-press a Buick. She could see their underwear—at least she could if she wanted to.

Johnny glanced back into the room where Candace's parents were sleeping. Could he make it to the window before Candace nabbed them? Not grabbed—nabbed. It was worth a try. But before he could move, Candace began to walk toward them.

Johnny froze.

Candace came closer. And closer.

Then she went into the bathroom and shut the door.

Knucklehead let out his breath. "It's like she didn't even see us."

"I don't think she did," Johnny whispered.

"Holy sleepwalker!" Knucklehead said.

Holy sleepwalker, indeed! The two

boys waited for Candace to come out of
the bathroom. Then they followed her
into the bedroom. They waited for
twenty minutes before they made their
next move. She seemed to be asleep, but
they had to be sure.

Very quietly they crept to the side of
the bed. Knucklehead pulled back the

covers an inch at a time. Johnny slowly untied the cape from around her neck. Next he tied on the fake one. Candace didn't stir, not even a twitch. "This is too easy for words, " he said to himself.

It was also too easy for cape stealing.

They crept down the hall holding their prize and left through the window. Once outside they ran. "I can't believe it!" Knucklehead yelled, jumping in the air. "We've got her cape!"

They stopped under a street light and looked it over. It looked and felt no different than the fake one. "I wonder what makes it super," Johnny said.

Knucklehead shrugged. "Try it on. See what happens."

Johnny put on the cape. "I don't feel

any different." He walked back and forth, twirled, jumped. Nothing out of the ordinary. "Hmmm . . . let me think . . . say 'On your mark, get set, go.'"

"On your mark, get set, go."

Johnny tore down the street. As fast as a speeding bullet. Maybe faster.

"Up, up, and away," he said when he reached a dead end. He was up and flying in one try. He zoomed back and forth above Knucklehead, who just stood there with his mouth open. While he was looking up, Johnny snatched him off the ground.

"What are you doing?" Knucklehead asked.

"Giving you a ride home."

The two partners in bullying zoomed

across the night sky. A few seconds later they were standing in Knucklehead's yard, after a pretty sloppy landing. Neither of them cared. They finally had what they'd always wanted—Candace Brinkwater's cape.

"Tomorrow we take over the school," Johnny said with a smile.

Soon he'd have to start working on his evil laugh.

THE CURSE OF MELVIN BEEDERMAN

Unfortunately, Johnny and Knucklehead couldn't take over the school just yet. They stole the cape on a Friday night. They'd have to wait until Monday to do any damage. In the meantime, Johnny would work on his landings. He could take off just fine. His landings needed help.

While Johnny was working out the kinks of his new life as bully-with-a-cape, the Spaz Brothers' Crime Spree was just getting started. They weren't the kind of bad guys to take the weekend off. They did, however, take frequent breaks to do cannonballs into their steaming hot Jacuzzi, while yelling things like "Geronimo!" and "Cowabunga!" It wasn't so much how you hit the water; it was what you yelled that counted.

But even before the weekend started, their very first crime was on the news.

"Wrinkled car thieves leave man stranded," said the reporter on channel 99. "Film at eleven."

Of course, the film at eleven just showed a man without a car. Major and Big were long gone. The point is, the Spaz Brothers were news. And it was only the beginning.

They wasted no time in committing
more crimes. Big crimes, little crimes . . .
you name it. They robbed a bank on
Century in broad daylight. They did this
by disguising themselves
as fire hydrants.

Why none of the bank employees thought this was suspicious, no one knew. The employees were later lectured by the police about this. "When you see fire hydrants with feet, that is a clue," one officer said, rolling his eyes. That bank would be ready next time.

The Spaz Brothers also robbed Crazy Larry's Good Time Tavern, where they served some of the best root beer in town, and the best pretzels, too.

With each crime the news spread. Things hadn't been so bad in Los Angeles since the McNasty Brothers broke out of prison—twice!

It was time for Candace Brinkwater to act. Melvin had left her in charge for this reason. People of the city were counting on her. After watching the news accounts about a couple wrinkled car thieves and some fire hydrant bank robbers, she launched herself from her front porch.

"Up, up, and away."

Crash!

She got to her feet and brushed herself off. Maybe she wasn't concentrating.

"Up, up, and away."

Splat!

Uh-oh. Two times in a row. She tried again.

Thud!

And again.

Kabonk!

"Holy Melvin curse!" Candace said. "I can't fly."

Holy Melvin curse, indeed! Little did she know that it was just the beginning of her troubles.

Candace spent most of the afternoon crashing, splatting, thudding, and kabonking. She tried jumping off the roof. She bounced on her neighbor's trampoline. Nothing worked.

"Melvin!" she yelled. "What have you done to me?"

EVIL TIMES AT HIGHMONT RIDGE

The Spaz Brothers continued their crime spree. They robbed, they mugged, they used bad language. They sprayed graffiti. And they celebrated with cannonballs into their Jacuzzi.

"Geronimo!"

Candace could do nothing. She couldn't fly. She couldn't outrun a skateboard, let alone a speeding bullet. And she couldn't see anyone's underwear— even when she tried! She thought it was

some kind of Melvin curse, of course. Little
did she know that she had a fake cape.

She rode the bus to school on Monday
morning with all the nonsuperhero kids.
She wore the cape like always, even
though she knew things had changed.

Maybe the Melvin curse would suddenly go away, and she wanted to be ready when it did.

Fortunately, the bullies weren't starting early that day. In fact, when Candace arrived at school, she didn't see the biggest bullies of them all—Johnny Fink and Knucklehead Wilson. This was good news. As long as she didn't have her powers, she was glad to have two less bullies to deal with.

Johnny and Knucklehead were late, nothing more. They were late because they had spent the morning going over their evil—almost sinister—plans. During class they looked at Candace, who sat on the nonbully side of the room. Soon it would be recess, and that's when Operation Get Candace Brinkwater would begin.

The recess bell rang at ten o'clock, and all the kids raced out onto the play- ground, Candace included.

"Hey, Candace," Johnny yelled. He stood at the far side of the school yard, near the buses.

Candace turned toward him. "What do you wa—"

Johnny Fink was wearing a cape exactly like hers.

"Nice underwear, Candace," he yelled.

Candace rubbed her eyes. Surely this had to be a dream. No, worse than that. It was a nightmare!

Johnny bent down and grabbed the rear end of the bus. "Watch this."

With one hand he lifted it over his head. He smiled his evil smile. He almost laughed an evil laugh.

Almost.

"Holy cape stealer!" Candace said. "This is terrible!"

Holy cape stealer, indeed! You better believe it.

Johnny crooked a finger. "Come over here, Candace."

Candace knew better. She turned and ran. But where to? If Johnny could see her underwear and lift a bus with one arm, he was probably as fast as a speeding bullet. Maybe faster.

Candace darted into the girls' bathroom. Fast as a speeding bullet or not, boys couldn't go into the girls' bathroom. For now she was safe.

CANDACE ON THE RUN

"Curses!" Johnny said. "She's in the girls' bathroom."

"Don't you mean drat?" Knucklehead asked.

"I mean curses. Can't you tell I'm getting more evil by the second?"

Knucklehead nodded. "So let's hear the evil laugh."

Johnny shook his head. "Not now. We have to get Candace."

It didn't take long for Johnny, former bully and now apprentice bad guy, to realize that he didn't have to obey the rules. After all, he was the strongest guy around. He marched straight for the girls' bathroom.

"You're going in the girls' room?" Knucklehead said, amazed. "Eww!"

Eww, indeed!

Johnny didn't care. He wanted to get Candace Brinkwater.

He kicked open the bathroom door. Then it happened. It came from deep inside him and burst from his mouth like a lion's roar. "Mwa ha ha."

Johnny had an evil laugh. And not just any evil laugh. It was a pretty darn good one.

Good enough to send shivers of terror down Candace's spine. She didn't stick around to see what evil things Johnny had in store for her. She dashed to the far side of the bathroom, dove through the window, and ran.

"Melvin, help!" she yelled. She headed for the school cafeteria. "Melvin, I'm in trouble."

But Melvin Beederman was in Las Vegas. He was taking a class called Stopping Trains Made Easy. Easy, his foot. There was nothing at all easy about stopping a speeding locomotive. At the moment he was having a difficult time with one. It was racing along at 66 miles per hour. And making a lot of noise—so much so that Melvin could not hear Candace's cries for help.

Melvin had superhero hearing, it's true, but that train was just too loud. Plus, his mind was racing. A train leaves Las Vegas going 66 miles per hour . . .

Screaming train in his ear, math problem in his head.

Holy distraction! He had no idea his partner in uncrime needed help.

Candace was on her own. But she didn't know this. She didn't know about the train, or the math problem. She kept yelling. "Help me, Melvin!"

Johnny was right behind her.

She darted into the cafeteria and ran for the refrigerator. Please let there be some bologna! The weakness was built into the cape. If she could find some bologna, her troubles would be over. She searched the shelves of the walk-in refrigerator. There was lots of cheese, lots of tuna salad, but no sign of the lunch meat she was looking for.

"Looking for something?" said a voice.

Candace turned and there was Johnny, standing in all his evil glory. "Mwa ha ha." And evil laugh, for that matter. He shut the door behind him and locked it. He walked forward. "Revenge time, Candace."

Candace shivered in fear. Or maybe she just shivered because it was cold.

After all, she was standing inside a refrigerator. She backed away, glancing once more to the shelves for bologna. There was none. Candace grabbed whatever she could get her hands on and threw it at Johnny. Tuna salad, cheese slices, Aunt Suzanne's Pudding Surprise. This did nothing to slow him down. It just made him smell like lunch.

Johnny grabbed her by the throat and squeezed.

"GASP." Candace turned blue . . . and it wasn't from cold.

Johnny squeezed harder and—

"Squeak squeak."

Johnny turned around. "What's that?"

Suddenly the refrigerator door tore from its hinges and crashed to the floor.

Johnny and Candace couldn't believe their eyes. It was a rat—a flying rat wearing a cape. It was Hugo, of course, and he was wearing the bit of cape that had torn off when Melvin jumped from the tree house door.

"Squeak squeak squeak."

This was rat talk for "Not so fast!" Or perhaps it was "I love kicking in doors."

The rat flew at Johnny, attacking with a karate chop to the head, a kick to the body, punches, and slaps. It even added a noogie. Johnny was too stunned to fight back. A rat with a cape? How can that be?

The rat continued to attack. Candace acted quickly. She reached out and

grabbed her cape, the real one. She put it on, tossing the fake one aside.

"Thanks," Candace said to the rat. "You must be Melvin's pet Hugo."

"Squeaker squeakity."

Candace didn't know exactly what the rat was saying. But it didn't matter. Right now she had a bad guy to beat up. Not bully—bad guy. "I'll take it from here," she told Hugo.

She did. She finished the job the rat had started, topping things off with the biggest noogie the world has ever seen. Then she dragged Johnny to the principal's office where he belonged.

Candace looked down at Melvin's rat, who had followed her. He must have heard her cries for help. The Superhero

Code said, Never Say No to a Cry for Help. Was it possible that Hugo knew the code?

"How can I ever thank you?" she asked.

"Squeaker squeakity squeak." This either meant "Just doing my job, ma'am," or "Got any crunchy pretzels on you?"

Hugo and Candace met again after school. They had some bad guys to catch.

"Up, up, and away." Candace launched herself, then turned to wait for her rat in uncrime.

Crash!

Splat!

Thud!

Kabonk!

"You've been spending too much time with Melvin Beederman," Candace said as they zoomed through the sky.

You can say that again!

ALL THAT SPAZ

The Spaz Brothers were unstoppable.
Each night they went out to do sinister
and devious deeds. Sometimes they did
them in broad daylight. Their lair was
filling up with expensive televisions,
stereos, great snack foods, and cold
hard cash. Occasionally they would get
warm hard cash . . . or cold soft cash. It
was all the same to Major Spaz and his
brother, Big.

They were just coming home from a

long day of robbing banks and jewelry stores, from stealing lunch money and using bad language—a tiring day for the partners in thievery.

"Can't wait to hit the Jacuzzi," Major told his brother as they began unloading their loot from the car.

"Me either." Big was trying to decide whether to say "Geronimo" or "Cowabunga" when he jumped in. "It's going to feel so good, Major."

"I know."

They walked into the lair and headed straight for the Jacuzzi. Suddenly they stopped. They were not alone.

"Holy breaking and entering!" Major said. The brothers stood with their mouths open.

Holy breaking and entering, indeed!

A girl and a rat were waiting for them inside. And not just inside the lair. They were inside the Jacuzzi!

"Care to join us, boys?" said the girl. This was Candace Brinkwater, of course. She turned to Hugo. "Please pass the pretzels."

Major and Big put on their evil smiles. Major added his not-so-evil laugh. "Hee ha hee ha ha hee." Beating up a girl and a rodent would be the perfect way to end the day. They dropped the loot and sprinted toward the girl and the rat, their large feet slapping the cement floor.

Pitter patter pitter patter pitter patter.

"Geronimo!" *Kersplash!*

"Cowabunga!" *Kersplash!*

"I'll take the ugly one," Candace said.

"Squeakity squeak?" This meant "They're both ugly." Or maybe it was "They're both ugly."

They smelled bad, too. And there were some extra bubbles in the Jacuzzi, which was suspicious.

Candace pinched her nose with one hand and punched Big with the other. Hugo pinched his nose with one paw and punched Major with the other. Two perfect punches and two unconscious bad guys. It was as simple as that. Maybe simpler.

"Good work, Hugo." Candace said as she dragged Big and Major out of the water. She and Hugo carried them to police headquarters.

The people of Los Angeles were safe once again. And they had Candace Brinkwater to thank for it . . . not to mention a pretzel-loving rat.

Melvin Beederman hugged his best friends, James and Margaret. "Fun times," he told them.

The Superhero Convention was over. It had been fun times, even though Melvin had placed thirty-ninth in the train-stopping competition. He didn't care. It was time to go home, and he was looking forward to seeing Hugo and doing math with Candace—and saving the world, of course. "See you later," he said.

Melvin took off. "Up, up, and away." Or at least he tried to.

Crash!
Splat!
Thud!
Kabonk!

On the fifth try he was up and flying and headed for Los Angeles. Once home, he met Candace at the library as usual.

"How'd it go, Candace? How'd you like saving the world all by yourself?"

Candace closed her math book and put it in her backpack. "Let's go get some pretzels and root beer, and I'll tell you all about it."

They went outside and launched themselves. Melvin joined his partner in uncrime on the fifth try, as usual, and they headed to Crazy Larry's, where they served the best pretzels in town. They sat at a table near the window and

Candace began her story—all about the cape caper, all about the Spaz Brothers, all about Hugo coming—

And that's when they heard it—someone yelling, someone crying for help.

"Guess I'll have to tell you my story some other time," Candace said, starting for the door.

Melvin nodded. "Right. Let's go, Candace."

They did. Candace's story would have to wait. Someone in Los Angeles was in trouble, and our two partners in uncrime would not disappoint them. They launched themselves outside Crazy Larry's.

At least Candace did. Melvin joined her after . . . well, you know.

WHO IS HUGO?

Hugo, as you might have expected, came from a long line of rats, although one of his uncles was a hippopotamus. If you're wondering how that is possible, just keep wondering—because the narrator will never tell you.

Like Melvin Beederman, Hugo was orphaned at an early age when his mother and kid sister, Harriet, were run over by a mob of raging shoppers. It was the day after Thanksgiving, the biggest shopping day of the year. The sales were too much to resist. Hugo begged his mom and sister to stay home that day. During a blowout sale? Was he kidding?

Splat!

Hugo's mom and sister never saw what hit them. But the narrator did. It was a pair of hiking boots, on sale for $24.95, which is a really good deal. They came with a three-year warranty.

And so for the first time in his life, Hugo was all alone. He wandered from rat hole to garbage heap, from garbage heap to rat hole. Nothing seemed to fit . . . until the day he climbed a tree and found a certain superhero who was willing to share his pretzels. As they say, a family that eats pretzels together, stays together. Hugo and Melvin aren't exactly family, but don't tell Hugo that. He's just glad Melvin doesn't like to shop.

 # THE SPAZ BROTHERS: THE EARLY YEARS

Major Spaz and his brother, Big, came from a long line of mad scientists. Parents, grandparents, aunts, uncles—you name it. If Spaz was their name, then taking over the world was their game. So it only made sense that Major and Big would sign up for Mad Scientist School as soon as they were old enough. But things did not go well. They were walking disaster areas, even when they were sitting!

Big Spaz blew up the school laboratory sixteen times during the first week of school. Major Spaz's science project came to life and ate professor Abraham B. Sinister, then consumed half a school bus before vanishing into the sewer, never to be seen again—although it sometimes can be heard playing harmonica late at night when the moon is full.

This was only the beginning of what has become known as Major and Big's Unexcellent Adventure. It was clear that they didn't have what it took to become mad scientists. They were mad enough, but they were a little short on noggin power.

Their mishaps are too numerous to name. Plus the narrator just finished writing five Melvin Beederman books and can barely type another word. He is also very busy eating Rocky Road ice cream. To make a long story short, the Spaz Brothers flunked out of Mad Scientist School and decided to enter Evil Bad Guy School instead.

And now, a superheroic excerpt from

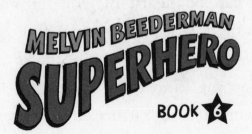

MELVIN BEEDERMAN SUPERHERO

BOOK 6

ATTACK OF THE VALLEY GIRLS

The two girls bit into the cookie made from the eggs contaminated by the mad scientist's evil potion. The change was immediate. Their eyes clouded over. Devious and sinister thoughts hit them all at once.

"How about we, like, take over the city?" Brittany said.

"That would be, like, totally cool!"

After school they headed to the mall to make plans. Neither of them had ever taken over a whole city before. This was exciting stuff!